THE CRAB PRINCE

AN ENTERTAINMENT FOR CHILDREN

RE-TOLD & ILLUSTRATED BY CHRISTOPHER MANSON

HENRY HOLT & CO. NEW YORK

Once, a beautiful girl named Rosella lived with her family in a little house near the sea.

The family was not rich; in fact, they were very poor. Rosella spent her days fetching water and carrying firewood and doing other chores. To make the work go faster, Rosella would sing little songs.

Rosella had the loveliest voice; she sounded like silver bells and warbling birds and laughing brooks, all at once. Whenever she sang, everyone felt better.

Now, Rosella was so beautiful that many young men came to ask for her hand in marriage . . . and many not-so-young men asked too.

They would say, "Dear, dear Rosella, you are so very beautiful! Will you marry me?"

She would say, "No, thank you, not today," because for some reason, she didn't like any of them enough to marry. Not even if they were rich.

Things went on like this for quite some time. Her parents didn't know what to do, and they were beginning to think that Rosella would never be married.

But this was not to be.

Near Rosella's house was an old well that no one used because it was brackish with seawater. One day, Rosella sat down by the well to rest. She began singing to pass the time.

And then a strange thing happened.

Out of the old well crawled the biggest crab that Rosella had ever seen! It had a bright green shell and lots of legs and two bulby eyes that wriggled around, this way and that. To tell you the truth, it was rather ugly, and when Rosella saw it she started to run away.

But the crab waved its claws *clickety-clack* and wriggled its eyes in circles. Rosella stopped. The crab was ugly and scary, but it was also funny, and a little sad too. Rosella decided right on the spot that she liked the giant crab.

So Rosella and the crab went home together. "Father, look what I have found in the old well!" she said.

Her father couldn't believe that she had brought home such an ugly thing. He said, "Daughter! A giant crab? What will the neighbors say? What will you do with it?"

"He will be my friend," said Rosella.

And so that was that.

After that, Rosella and the crab were together all the time. The crab helped Rosella carry loads and loads of firewood, and buckets and buckets of water.

When the chores were done, Rosella would skip away to play her mandolin. And when Rosella danced and sang, the crab would wave its claws *clickety-clack* and wriggle its eyes, and hop up and down and beat a tambourine in time to the music. To tell you the truth, the crab looked very funny.

They had a wonderful time together.

But Rosella's parents didn't think it was proper for their daughter to spend so much time with a giant crab—and such an ugly one too. All the neighbors said it was very odd.

Rosella didn't care about that. But she had noticed something strange about the crab.

very day, just at the hour of noon, the crab would dive down into the old well and not return until three o'clock.

Rosella watched and watched, but she could never see what it was doing down there. Finally she said, "I just have to see for myself!"

So the girl took off her skirt and her apron and her jacket and her shoes, and put them in a neat pile.

Then she dove down into the old well.

Down and down she swam. At the very bottom, off in a corner, she found a small, dark hole, and she swam right into it.

She swam and swam and swam, until she could hold her breath no longer. Just when she thought she might never breathe again . . .

She popped up out of the water. Rosella was in a gloomy cavern under the sea. It was dark and damp and cold. Overhead Rosella could hear the fishes gurgling in the water, the waves crashing on the shore, and the sea gulls crying in the air.

Then she saw the crab. It was scuttling along after a strange old woman. Rosella knew the old woman had to be a ghula. Now, I am here to tell you that a ghula is a nasty creature who knows a lot of magic, and even though Rosella had never seen one before, she knew enough to hide.

Under her arm the ghula held a wriggly fish that shone like gold, and she croaked in a terrible, creaky old voice, "Come along, my boy, come along!"

hen Rosella saw the ghula touch the crab's hard, green shell with the golden fish and say, "Come out, come out of your shell!"

And the ugly crab was changed into a handsome young man!

"Now!" screeched the ghula to the young man. "Sing me a song, or there's no supper for you!"

So the young man sang a song for the ghula, and it was one of Rosella's songs. It was a happy little song, but the young man wept as he sang it.

Rosella was so moved by the young man's tears, and the way he looked, and the way he sang her song, that she fell in love with him right on the spot!

Then the ghula said, "Very, very well! I am pleased! Now you may have your supper!" And in another chamber there was a table set for a banquet, and the two sat down to eat their fill.

But still, the young man was very sad.

Soon the ghula, who had eaten too much and made a big mess, fell asleep inside a large dish. But she never let go of the wriggly golden fish.

Rosella ran out of her hiding place. The young man was surprised to see her.

"Rosella!" he whispered, "How did you get here? You must leave right away, or the ghula will kill us both!"

"I swam after you," said Rosella. "Are you a man or a crab?"

The young man sighed. "You see me now as I really am. Long ago, I was sailing on the sea and my ship was wrecked upon a rock. The ghula snatched me from the water and brought me here. Now, I am in her power—an ugly green crab, except for the few hours when I swim down here to sing for my supper."

"How terrible!" said Rosella. "Is there no way to save you?"

"The wriggly golden fish is the secret to the ghula's spell, but the ghula always keeps it with her. Only someone who loves me enough to die for me can break the spell."

"I am that someone!" said Rosella. Then she ran out of the chamber and swam home again.

By the time the sun came up the next morning, she knew what she would do.

The next day Rosella took her mandolin down to the seashore. She walked along listening to the sea gulls crying in the air, the waves crashing on the shore, and the fishes gurgling in the water.

Then she played her mandolin and sang as sweetly as she possibly could. And that was very sweetly, indeed!

Down below, in her dark and drippy caverns, the ghula heard Rosella's music and quick as a wink, she popped up out of a hole on the beach to listen. That's when Rosella gave a big yawn and stopped playing.

"I'm so very tired!" she said loudly. "I think I will go home now!"

"Young maiden!" cried the ghula. "Do not stop playing your mandolin and singing your songs! I must hear more!"

"Well," said Rosella. "Even though I am very, very tired, I will make more music to please you . . . but you must give me a present in return."

"I will give you anything you wish!" said the ghula.

So Rosella played and sang, and played and sang, and played and sang until it was late in the day. Such beautiful music Rosella made!

V ery, very well!" said the ghula. "I am very, very pleased!"

"Then, you must give me the present you have promised," said Rosella, her heart beating very fast. "You must give me all the gold I wish!"

"Very well," said the ghula, and she dipped her hand into the sea and brought out heaps of sunken treasures. Piles of bright gold glittered in the sun. "All this is yours," she said.

But Rosella said, "No, thank you, not today. You agreed to give me all the gold I wish . . . and *all* the gold I wish to have is that wriggly golden fish you carry."

"No! Not the wriggly golden fish!" cried the ghula. "Take these beautiful jewels, instead!" And she dipped her hand into the sea again, and brought out strings of lustrous pearls and dazzling gems, silver vessels, and all manner of precious things. How they sparkled!

But Rosella said, "No, thank you, not today. I wish only to have that wriggly golden fish!"

Well, the ghula was vexed beyond measure at this. "Then you have only to fetch it!" she screeched, and the spiteful creature threw the wriggly golden fish into the sea!

osella dove right into the sea. She swam and swam and swam after the precious golden fish.

The ghula made the wind blow and the waves roll higher, and the wriggly golden fish swam farther out to sea.

But Rosella didn't give up.

Soon she was very tired and the shore was very far behind her.

But Rosella kept on swimming.

The ghula made more wind and more waves, and more wind and more waves, and more wind and more waves!

But Rosella kept on going.

At last, far out to sea, Rosella, with her last bit of strength, reached out . . . and caught the tip of the tail of the wriggly golden fish in her hand.

And the biggest wave of all came crashing down!

Rosella tumbled down under the waves—she sank deeper and deeper and deeper into the water.

But she held on to that fish.

And the water became darker and colder, and darker and colder, and darker and colder!

But she didn't let go of that fish.

"I'm going to die, just as my love said I would," she thought sadly.

But still she didn't lose that fish!

Then her feet touched something. "I've reached the bottom of the sea at last," she thought.

But she was wrong.

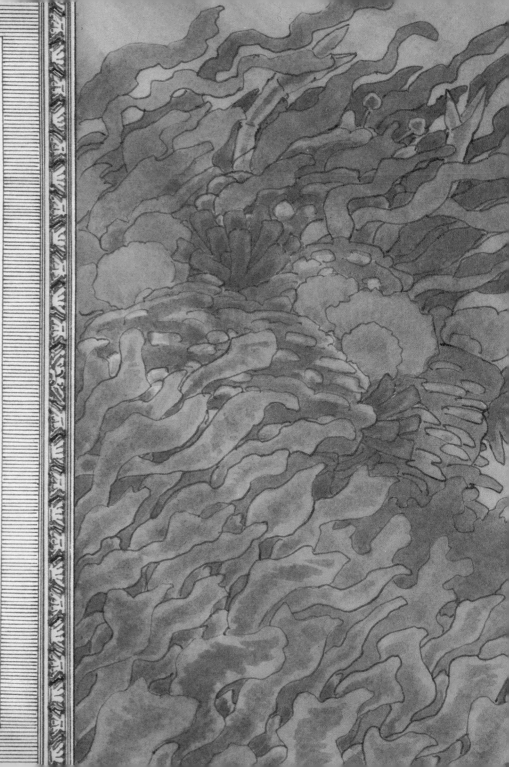

Under her feet was her friend the crab. He lifted her up on his back and carried her through the water. The water became brighter and warmer, and brighter and warmer, and brighter and warmer until . . . they reached the air and sunlight again.

The crab swam strongly through the waves and carried Rosella safely all the way back to shore.

And you can easily believe me when I tell you that she held on to that wriggly golden fish all the way!

When they reached the shore, Rosella touched the crab's hard green shell with the golden fish and said, "Come out, come out of your shell!"

And the ugly crab changed into the handsome young man, right on the spot. Then she threw the fish back into the sea, and it swam away and was never seen again.

The ghula saw what had happened, and she was so vexed that she hopped up and down, and up and down, and up and down until she fell into her hole, and *she* was never seen again!

And no one was sorry about that.

The young man knelt before Rosella and said, "Dear, dear Rosella! You have saved me, and I thank you a thousand, thousand times! But you must tell no one of what has happened. Good-bye!"

And with that the handsome young man jumped to his feet and ran off down the beach as fast as he could.

"Wait!" cried Rosella, "You haven't told me your name!"

But he was already gone.

The next day Rosella sat quietly and sadly at home. She had told no one of what had happened, so her parents had no idea why she was so unhappy.

Suddenly there was a sound.... It was music!

It was drums and trumpets and fiddles, and they were all playing one of Rosella's little songs. Rosella and her family ran outside. A grand parade of musicians and servants and soldiers was marching up to their little house.

Leading them all was the handsome young man wearing a golden crown.

"Good sir!" he called out to Rosella's father, "Know that I am Prince Florian, and I have come to ask for your daughter's hand in marriage!" The trumpeters blew a great fanfare on their trumpets, and everyone waited to hear the answer.

But Rosella's father said, "You may as well go right back home, young man! My daughter has never said yes to anyone before, and I think she never will."

Much to his astonishment, Rosella smiled and took Prince Florian's hand. "This is the man I will marry," she said, "This is my crab prince!"

And the trumpeters blew another great fanfare on their trumpets!

As you might imagine, Rosella and Prince Florian had a great, grand and glorious wedding celebration, and everyone for miles around was invited.

It was so wonderful that the people are still talking about it today.

Prince Florian gave Rosella beautiful robes to wear and a crown of gold, and they went to live in a beautiful palace in the prince's country.

And right now they are living happily together, having a wonderful time. And, if you are ever in their country, you can hear Prince Florian and Princess Rosella singing happy songs together.

Published by Henry Holt and Company, Inc., 115 West 18th Street, New York, New York 10011.
Published simultaneously in Canada by Fitzhenry & Whiteside Ltd., 195 Allstate Parkway, Markham, Ontario L3R 4T8.

Library of Congress Cataloging-in-Publication Data
Manson, Christopher.   The crab prince: a Venetian tale / retold and illustrated by Christopher Manson.
Summary: A retelling of the Italian folktale about the brave and beautiful Rosella and her one true love.
ISBN 0-8050-1215-X (alk. paper)   [1. Folklore—Italy.]   I. Title.   PZ8.1.M2985Cr   1991   398.2—dc20   90-26626   [E]

Henry Holt books are available at special discounts for bulk purchases for sales promotions, premiums,
fund-raising, or educational use. Special editions or book excerpts can also be created to specification.

First edition   Printed in the United States of America on acid-free paper. ∞

1   3   5   7   9   10   8   6   4   2

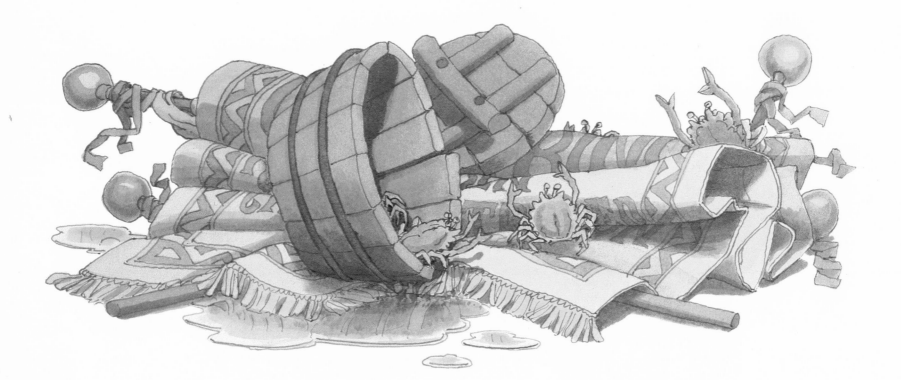